The Problem with NOT Being Scared of Kids

Dan Richards

Illustrated by

Robert Neubecker

BOYDS MILLS PRESS

AN IMPRINT OF HIGHLIGHTS

Honesdale, Pennsylvania

For Mom
—DR

For Ruth, Iz, and Jo
—RN

Text copyright © 2015 by Dan Richards
Illustrations copyright © 2015 by Robert Neubecker

Boyds Mills Press
An Imprint of Highlights
815 Church Street
Honesdale, Pennsylvania 18431
Printed in Malaysia

ISBN: 978-1-62979-102-9
Library of Congress Control Number: 2014958540
First edition
Production by Sue Cole
The text of this book is set in Zemke Hand ITC.
The illustrations are drawn with pen and ink on watercolor paper and
colored on a Macintosh.

10 9 8 7 6 5 4 3 2 1

The problem with **NOT** being scared of kids is . . .

...they don't want to **hang** out with us.

Sleepovers end early.

Bus rides are **boring**.

Always being "it" grows old.

Holidays get personal.

Being **helpful**...

doesn't really help.

Sharing is a **letdown**.

Claws and **crafts** don't mix.

Snowball fights become **one-sided**.

Even when all you want is to **fit in,**
you don't.

And just when you're ready to **give up** . . .

...**SOMEONE** comes along who changes everything.

No problem.